POLLY'S PUFFIN

Sarah Garland

Greenwillow Books
New York

Polly did not like shopping with Baby Jim.

He never stopped throwing things.

One day, when they stopped to have
a cup of tea,

Polly let Jim play with her puffin,
for a treat.

This was a big mistake.

First Jim hugged it.

Then he kissed it.

Then, with all his might and main he threw it...

straight into the hood
of the man sitting behind him.

Never noticing the puffin, the man walked quickly through the door.

Polly leaped to her feet.

They ran through the fashion department.

They went up the escalator – but
the man was going down.

They left the shop just in time to see...

the man turning a corner.

When they reached the next street
he had disappeared completely.

They searched the market.

They asked at the library.

They hunted through the pet shop.

At last they turned for home.

Polly thought she would never
see her puffin again.

But she was wrong!

And the next time they went shopping,
Polly thought she might leave her
puffin safely at home.

Library of Congress Cataloging-in-Publication Data

Garland, Sarah
Polly's puffin / Sarah Garland
p.   cm.
Summary: While they are in a restaurant, Baby Jim
tosses his sister Polly's toy puffin
into the hood of a stranger's coat, and he
leads them on a merry chase through the city.
ISBN 0-688-08748-5.   ISBN 0-688-08749-3 (lib. bdg.)
[1. Lost and found possessions—Fiction.
2. City and town life—Fiction.
3. Babies—Fiction.   4. Toys—Fiction.]
I. Title.   PZ7.G18414Pm 1989
[E]—dc19   88-24348   CIP   AC